Lavender Moon

Troon Harrison
Eugenie Fernandes

Annick Press • Toronto • New York

Three times each week the late-night bus shudders to a stop before the New Moon Café. Yawning passengers climb out. Bells tinkle on the café door.

This is the busiest time of Lavender Moon's long day. In winter the passengers want minestrone soup and hot coffee. In summer they ask for cherry pie and cold fruit juice. Lavender Moon hustles and bustles. The cash register rattles and rings.

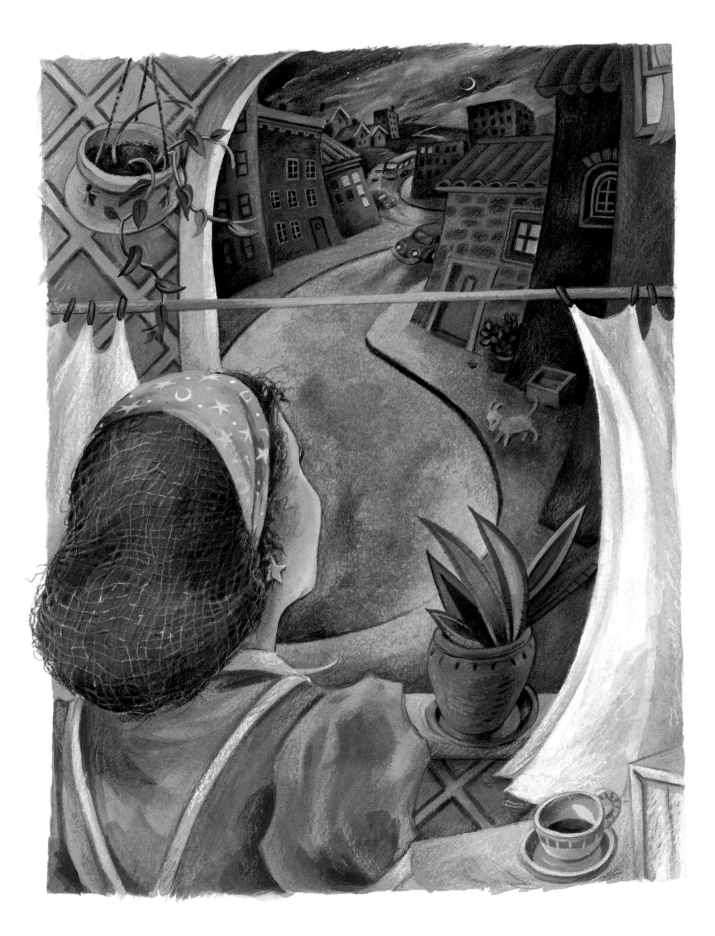

At ten-thirty the driver, Toby Swan, rises to his feet. "Time's flying by!" he calls. The door bells tinkle again. Lavender Moon watches the bus roar away. Its lights fade into the darkness of the countryside.

As she mops the floor, Lavender thinks how mysterious the late-night bus is. She has never seen the places it comes from, or the ones that it roars away to.

Twenty years is long enough to spend cutting pies and grilling sandwiches, she decides as she hangs the *Closed* sign on the door.

When the bus comes again, Lavender pours Toby Swan a coffee.

"Mr. Swan," she says, "I have decided to ride on your bus. I want to discover where the road goes."

"But haven't you heard?" asks Toby. "The bus is not going to run any more."

"Whatever do you mean?" cries Lavender Moon.

"I am too old to be rushing around," explains Toby. "I am looking for a place to settle down and stay."

Lavender Moon is horrified. No more passengers to eat her soup and pies! No more chances for her to ride the late-night bus! She will never find out where the road goes. She has waited too long.

"I am tired of pie crust and dirty forks," Lavender Moon grumbles. "I am tired of table-cloths and soup spoons."

As she cleans the counter, she begins to make a plan. When she hangs up the *Closed* sign, she is smiling.

Then something happens that has never happened before. The late-night bus stops at the café door early one morning. No passengers climb out, only Toby Swan. He hands the bus keys to Lavender.

"Have a good trip," he tells her.

Lavender hands the café keys to Toby. "I hope you'll be happy here," she says.

"Oh, yes," agrees Toby. "I am going to open a hardware store. It's what I've always dreamed of."

Lavender Moon climbs the four steps
into the bus. The engine starts with a roar.
"Goodbye!" calls Toby Swan.

Lavender Moon drives down the street, headed for the
country. She drives over green hills and waves to farmers.
She crosses sparkling rivers and waves to boaters.

In unfamiliar towns Lavender Moon buys tall ice cream sundaes. She dances on the grass while the band plays. On warm summer evenings she swoops round and around on painted horses. Fireworks blossom in the sky.

There are so many towns to visit, and so much to see.

Sometimes Lavender stops by a shin-
ing lake. She does a cannon-ball off the
diving platform and scares the crayfish.

She paddles around on a yellow crocodile. Then
she remembers that there are other places to see.
She has not reached the end of the road yet.

It is peaceful in the desert. Lavender explores caves and digs for dinosaur bones. She drifts through the sky in a hot-air balloon.

Finally, she climbs back into her bus. I don't know where I am going, she thinks, but I will know when I get there.

In the mountains Lavender Moon
bounces down rapids in a raft. She wears
new boots to climb with mountain goats.

This is such fun that she almost forgets
her bus. Then she remembers she has
not reached the end of her journey.

One afternoon, when the café is very far behind, Lavender Moon reaches the ocean. She walks barefoot on warm sand and flies a kite above the tossing waves. *This* is the end of the road, she thinks. *This* is the place for me.

Lavender Moon buys a house where the village and the dunes meet. It has a weather vane shaped like a ship. There is sand on the kitchen floor. A skinny cat hides beneath the verandah.

"I've arrived home," Lavender tells the cat. "We can share the house. I'll call you Fishwhiskers."

Toby Swan is pleased to get a postcard.

"My friend Lavender Moon is happy by the ocean, but I'm happy right here," he tells the mailman. "This is the place for me."

Soon his first customer of the day will arrive. Toby forgets all about the ocean and begins to organize tools.

Lavender Moon starts to paint. She paints children splashing and dogs playing.

Lavender Moon buys a surf-board. Whenever the waves are just right, she wooshes towards shore in a bright bathing-suit.

All summer she is perfectly happy.

When summer ends, it gets too wet to paint and too rough to surf. Lavender notices how quiet her house is. The wind makes a lonely sound. She remembers how much people liked her soup and pies.

"Lavender Moon," they used to say, "no one can cook like you can!"

Now she has no one to cook for but herself.

I can't go back, she thinks. My café is a hardware store.

While the rain falls and her chair rocks, Lavender thinks of a new plan.

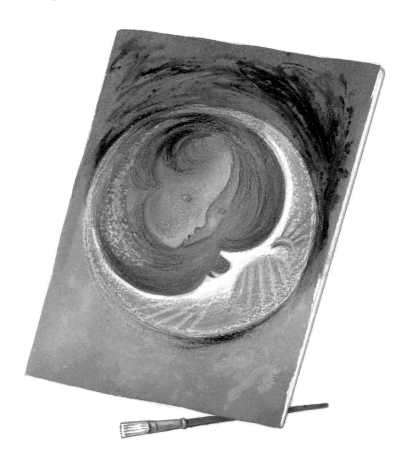

When she calls Forrest Cedar, the carpenter, he begins work right away. Soon he has taken all the seats from the late-night bus. He whistles as he builds counters and tables. Lavender Moon folds napkins, counts forks and hangs up paintings.

Now, Lavender Moon paints
pictures some days. Other days,
if the waves are just right, she
heads down to the beach with
her surfboard.

On all the rest of the days,
Lavender Moon drives her café
along the coast. She stops wher-
ever the view is best. She serves
clam chowder, fried fish, oysters,
chips and cold soda pop.

"Lavender Moon," the people
say, "no one can cook seafood as
well as you can!"

They ask for second helpings
—and sometimes they even buy
a painting.

The cash register rattles and
rings. Lavender Moon hustles and
bustles and is perfectly happy.

Fishwhiskers grows plump
and dreams about haddock.

For Shelly, who knows the bus,
and for Jane, who knows Lavender Moon
T.H.

For Carolyn, who is following the road
E.F.

©1997 Troon Harrison (text)
©1997 Eugenie Fernandes (art)
Design by Sheryl Shapiro and Eugenie Fernandes

Annick Press Ltd.

Annick Press gratefully acknowledges the support of the
Canada Council and the Ontario Arts Council.

Cataloguing in Publication Data
Harrison, Troon
Lavender Moon

ISBN 1-55037-455-9 (bound)   ISBN 1-55037-454-0 (pbk.)

I. Fernandes, Eugenie, 1943-   II. Title.

PS8565.A6587L38 1997   jC813'.54   C97-930610-8
PZ7.H37La 1997

The art in this book was rendered in gouache, oil pastels and coloured pencils.
The text was typeset in Esprit.

Distributed in Canada by: Published in the U.S.A. by Annick Press (U.S.) Ltd.
Firefly Books Ltd.   Distributed in the U.S.A. by:
3680 Victoria Park Avenue   Firefly Books (U.S.) Inc.
Willowdale, ON   P.O. Box 1338
M2H 3K1   Ellicott Station
                                       Buffalo, NY 14205

Printed and bound in Canada by Friesens.

E
HAR

Harrison, Troon.

Lavender Moon.

$16.95

YPVE55282

E
HAR

Harrison, Troon.

Lavender Moon.

YPVE55282

$16.95

DATE | BORROWER'S NAME

K-2 | Allison Mc B